WASIM THE WANDERER

Wasim the Wanderer copyright © Frances Lincoln Limited 2007
Text copyright © Chris Ashley 2007
Illustrations copyright © Kate Pankhurst 2007

First published in Great Britain in 2007 and in the USA in 2008 by
Frances Lincoln Children's Books, 4 Torriano Mews,
Torriano Avenue, London NW5 2RZ

www.franceslincoln.com

First paperback edition published in 2007

British Library Cataloguing in Publication Data available on request

ISBN: 978-1-84507-745-7

Printed in Singapore

1 3 5 7 9 8 6 4 2

WASIM THE WANDERER

Chris Ashley

F

FRANCES LINCOLN
CHILDREN'S BOOKS

Chapter One

Teamwork 10,000! Every Wednesday,
a real football coach – not just
Mr Abbott the headteacher, but a
real one – was coming to teach football.

Wasim Ahmed loved football –
loved watching it, loved talking about
it, loved collecting the cards and most
of all loved playing it. But he hadn't
done the 'minter' cough in assembly
when Mr Abbott reminded them all to
bring their kits because Teamwork 10,000

was starting tomorrow.

"Well, it was somebody," stormed Mrs Scott. Somebody had *let the whole class down.* So now here they all were, Junior S, on the hall floor glaring at Charles, while Mrs Scott was sitting on the PE bench sipping her playtime coffee and marking spellings. She didn't mind being here at all – it was their own time they were all wasting.

Charles was always finding new ways of saying something was good. For the last few weeks it had been pretending to cough but really saying 'minter'. It annoyed Mrs Scott. Ben pointed at him, hoping Miss Scott would see but that it wouldn't be counted as telling. But Mrs Scott carried on ticking and crossing.

"You tell on him, Wasim," Donna hissed. But Wasim wasn't worried about missing a break, not today anyway. So it was left for Ben to nudge Charles and Donna to do the glaring. It seemed to be working.

"Miss?"

"Yes, Charles?"

"Can I go to toilet, Miss?"

"No, Charles."

"Miss?"

"Yes, Charles?"

"It was me, Miss."

Mrs Scott made a big show of closing the spelling books.

"At last! Well, Charles, you can spend the rest of the break practising not letting our class down in assembly. And the rest of you, I'm sorry that your time was wasted by this silly boy. Out you go."

"Miss. It was me as well, Miss."

The whole class stopped looking like sinned-against saints to stare at Wasim. No it wasn't. Wasim hadn't done anything… not this time.

"Right then, Wasim, you've let down our class as well. Sit down next to Charles and turn your rude backs to each other, please."

"Minter," Charles whispered.

Yeah, minter, Wasim thought. One more break away from Robert Bailey.

Chapter Two

The trouble had started on Monday.
By then everyone had signed up for
Teamwork. Mrs Scott's class had gone
football mad and the upper junior
playground was a no-go area for
anything that wasn't round or couldn't
be kicked or headed.

Mrs Smart the dinner lady was
quite round but…

"I didn't see her," Wasim explained
to Mr Abbott, as the ball he had sent

rocketing into the dinner lady was put in the staffroom cupboard.

"So?" Wasim had said when he got back outside. But 'so' wasn't much good to Robert Bailey from Year Six. It was his ball and the look in his eyes told Wasim to stay well out of his way... well out!

He managed it until afternoon break, but then Year Six came charging down the corridor and in the middle of them all was Bailey.

Somehow Wasim had never noticed how big he was before. He was big.

And Wasim had never really noticed how quickly a corridor got emptied. Now it was just him, Bailey and two of Bailey's mates.

Wasim felt real fear. His legs buzzed.

It made him want to go to the toilet and his heart beat so hard it almost hurt.

He needed to say something about the ball but he had to swallow first and he couldn't. Then he saw a fist, and he ducked and waited. Nothing. There was nothing. Bailey was scratching the back of his head as if that was why he had moved his arm.

The Year Sixes were laughing and Wasim was crawling on the floor trying to find his glasses, sure the sound of that laughing was hurting just as much as the fist would have.

It had happened twice since then. Whichever way Wasim went, Bailey would seem to be there with Darren Forbes or Ian Cousins and then he'd

pull back a fist and wait for Wasim
to duck and there would always be
the laughing. The nasty laughing.
Sometimes Wasim was sure Bailey
wasn't going to hit him. But he wasn't
sure enough.

"Tell Miss," Ben said, but Wasim
shook his head, hoping it wouldn't
force a tear of rage and helplessness
out. Miss couldn't tell someone off for
scratching their head, could she? And
you couldn't tell her how it made you
feel like nothing, how you couldn't care
less about your spelling test on Friday
or being told off for not listening at the
mosque. You couldn't worry about
things that used to be important,
like whether Miss would let you be
Pharaoh in the Egyptians assembly.

No, Ben didn't understand. Nobody would. You just couldn't tell someone that another boy kept finding you on your own and scratching his head instead of punching you, just so that you would crouch and hold your head and look babyish. And that because of this boy you'd felt so sick for three days you couldn't even eat the Snickers bar Dad brought home every night. You couldn't tell them you felt like nothing, could you? Just a piece of nothing.

• • •

So now Wasim was in the hall, safe for another twenty minutes. Nobody would do anything with Mrs Scott around. Maybe by tomorrow and

Teamwork 10,000 day, Bailey would
have his ball back and would have
forgotten all about it.

"Right, you two. You can stay with
your backs to each other in silence.
I'm just popping to the, err, *staffroom*."

Mrs Scott's footsteps died away and
mingled with the shouts and screams
of the playground.

"Minter!" Charles coughed again.

"Minter," Wasim coughed back but his heart wasn't in it. His eyes were darting between the two hall doors, working out how quickly he could get through one of them if Bailey decided to strike.

Chapter Three

Wednesday, Teamwork 10,000 day.

Wasim was up at six. Dad was up but Wasim didn't want to talk. By twenty past he was standing at the door with his ball.

"What are you doing?"

"I'm just going to practise at the garages."

Dad laughed. "Even Mr Holloway would give you a red card at this time in the morning."

Wasim went back upstairs and
packed his PE kit again. He always
played football down by the garages.
Sometimes on his own, just hammering
the ball against old Mr Holloway's
clanging garage for hours. Or
sometimes – and best of all – with Atif,
Shamaila and Dad. It would be Wasim
and Atif (United) against Dad and

Shamaila (Chelsea). They were happy times. No worries about anything. Just laughing, and Mr Holloway waving his stick if Shamaila scored or if Wasim managed to get round Dad and unleash one of his specials.

Today wouldn't be the garages though!

Wasim checked the boots he was borrowing from Atif again and for a few pain-free seconds his mind was back on its usual subject, football. And Teamwork 10,000 was real football. 10,000 children all over the country were going to get real coaching and these next few weeks, it was their school's turn. Real football. Maybe he was too old for the garages now, anyway.

Wasim didn't know how he got
through the day, but he did – with no
playtimes either. He found a job
helping Mrs Caulfield the caretaker,
just until he was sure Bailey had his
ball back, and then at dinner time
he got himself kept in for not working
hard enough with Mrs Hussein, his
special teacher.

Finally half past three came and
it was time to get changed. Wasim had
to show he was a real footballer now.
He took out his shining white PE vest
with its razor creases and folded it
neatly on his desk. Then he allowed
himself a look round to see if anyone
else knew how to do it properly.
They did. Filling every centimetre of
Mrs Scott's usually neat classroom were

the shirts, shorts, socks, shinpads and sweatbands of every football club you could think of.

Charles was already showing off. "Which one will I need, Miss? United home, United away, United anniversary or United Europe?"

Wasim was pleased when Mrs Scott's glare seemed to say she didn't care.

"What have you got, Waz?" Charles was still going on.

Wasim looked at his PE vest. He was the only one without a proper kit.

"White."

"White? What, Spurs, United away, England?"

Wasim concentrated on tying up Atif's laces and hoped that having black boots instead of the silver, gold and blue ones that the other children were all wearing wouldn't cause more show-ups.

Everyone was too busy to notice
though and at least Wasim was first out.
Freezing spikes of hail stung his head
and the cold made bumps appear all
over his arms and legs.

Slowly the field filled up with
screaming, charging, mud-kicking boys
and determined-looking girls. Too many
people for even Bailey to try anything.
Finally Mr Abbott and
Miss Pollitt, the Year Three
teacher, came out. They
were followed by a huge,
fit-looking man in a proper
England anorak. He was
carrying a net full of
leather footballs and
an armful of blue
traffic cones.

The big man
blew a whistle.
He was in
charge tonight,
not Mr Abbott.

"I'm John
Dawson, and
I'm coach for
Teamwork 10,000." Everyone cheered.
"Now I expect some of your dads might
have told you about my playing days at
Bury? Charlton Athletic..?" No dads had,
so Mr Dawson had to cough and carry
on. "Right, er, now I'm going to split
you up into little groups and then we'll
see how good we can get you after
Teamwork 10,000."

Wasim exchanged a thumbs-up
with Wing Ho.

"I said, Teamwork 10,000!" Mr Dawson cupped a hand to his ear.

"TEAMWORK 10,000!" they all had to holler back, Wasim the loudest.

"Right, line up and we'll do a warm-up, then I'll put you into groups and you, you son," Mr Dawson pointed at Wasim, "you go and put a jumper on under that vest. You can't shiver and play football at the same time."

The whistle blew again and there was a stampede for the far goal post. The children all had to run while Wasim hunched his shoulders and walked back into school to find his jumper. It took him twenty minutes. He got told off for leaving mud in the corridor, had to find Mrs Scott, then get the classroom unlocked and put his jumper on.

By the time he got back out, the dribbling and passing games were over and Mr Dawson had set up lots of little matches where you were only supposed to touch the ball two times. Wasim had no chance to show how good he was because he had to join a group of Year Three children and it was obvious Mr Dawson wasn't bothered with this group at all.

Miss Pollitt, who was nice and knew about football, came and said 'good' a couple of times and Wasim tried to get interested but it was a boring, cold, stupid game. What was worse, people kept booting the ball past the little blue cones on to the other pitches where kids like Wing Ho, Ben and Charles were playing.

Charles was glowing in England's red away kit. "Why are you in the babies' group?" he kept asking.

At last it was all over. The Year Sixes, allowed to stay for an extra session, got ready for a proper match while the younger ones had a last screech of 'Teamwork 10,000' (Wasim didn't join in) and went to look for proud mums and dads. Wasim was meant to be going home with Charles but Charles had done so well that he'd been asked to play in the Year Six match.

Mr Abbott found Wasim shivering on the touchline.

"What are you doing?"

"Waiting for Charles," said Wasim.

"Well, come and have a run about in this game, then. You know Mr Dawson doesn't like to see people shivering."

Mr Abbott winked and Wasim, his tummy rolling over, sprinted on to the pitch as fast as his legs would carry him. He would have to get in quickly – it would be dark soon. He rushed over to where a pile of bodies booted the ball while Mr Dawson stood shaking his head.

"No, no, no... Positions, space... don't follow the ball..."

A whistle blew and they all had to stop while Mr Dawson put them back into positions.

"On the wing, son... there."

So that was where Wasim stood, on the wing. There was no chance of the ball coming, and he'd had enough. Maybe he really was no good and the skills he seemed to have down at the garages didn't count. He hated Teamwork 10,000. He hated everything and he started kicking the tops off frozen wormcasts. TOE SMELL 10,000. TOILET 10,000. Wasim booted another wormcast – and then it happened.

"Oy, Wasim!"

"Ahmed, Ahmed."

But Wasim wasn't listening because he could see it now. Between the splats of mud on his glasses and between the England, United and Chelsea kits he could see the ball. It had bounced, it had skidded and now it was rolling towards him. After twenty-five minutes Wasim, standing by the touchline, was going to get the ball.

"Wasim, Wasim to me!"

It was his.

"Mine, Wasim… Waz! Back door, Waz… Wasim!"

But Wasim closed his ears and as the ball slurped the last few centimetres he did what he'd done a thousand, million times down at the garages… He watched it, watched it, watched it…. Last look up and yes, the keeper was off his line, he planted his left foot next to the ball, short back swing with his right and.. and he hit it… Wasim really hit it.

BHOUF!

"Oh, Wasim!"

"So?" Wasim started to say, as the ball flew through the air. He knew he shouldn't have shot from there. But he hadn't had a touch for nearly half an hour and Teamwork 10,000 had been rubbish and he wasn't in a proper kit and he was fed up with ducking, crouching and dropping his glasses. So he'd had a go. So?

The shouting stopped and there was silence over the school field. Even the seagulls picking up the playground crisps stopped their noisy support.

And then he knew it.

He knew it had been good. The seagulls, the shouts and the cars all started again while Wasim watched

the ball hurtle through the freezing
evening air and blast, still rising,
over the head of a defender in a bib.

The goalkeeper stopped doing
practice karate kicks and tried to dive
but he missed it by a mile. He had to
watch while the whole goal wobbled,
the ball hit the back of the net and
then snaked down with that slippery
noise you heard at the start of
Match of the Day.

"Wake up, keeper!"

There had only been a few more minutes after that and Wasim's head hurt with all the people who kept roughing his hair and saying, "Top one, Waz!" Especially as it meant that their team won 3:2.

But Wasim wasn't enjoying it.

He had one eye on the goalkeeper who was doing karate kicks again and whose eyes were blazing like floodlights out of the gloom. Robert Bailey, the school goalkeeper, was not happy.

Chapter Four

Get away quickly. That was what
Wasim would have to do.

"You two, could you stay behind
for a minute?"

Good. It was Bailey and Charles
Mr Dawson wanted, so there would
be time to escape before Bailey got out.
He joined in the last Teamwork 10,000
chant and then began a run to the
school gate.

"Oy!"

Wasim carried on.

"Oy … Back!" There was a whistle
that could only have come from
Mr Dawson and Wasim had to slow
down. "Help me with these, will you?"
And with the rest of the crowd drifting
away and leaving him worryingly alone,
Wasim had to help Charles and a silent
Robert Bailey carry the football stuff
to Mr Dawson's big white car.

Then he asked them, "How would
you like a trial for Woodley Wanderers?
It's a club I run on Saturdays and
Sundays."

Wasim looked at Charles and then
caught sight of the first real smile he'd
ever seen on Robert Bailey's face.
Mr Dawson didn't have to explain who
Woodley Wanderers were. They were

the top youth team in the town. They were in the *Advertiser* every week, standing next to one cup or another. If you played you were known as a Wanderer and if you were a Wanderer you were a king!

"No promises," Mr Dawson was saying. "It's only a trial. But you, son – Wos, Wis... Ahm?"

"Armpit," came a nasty whisper from behind Wasim, but no one else heard.

"Ahmed," Wasim managed to say.

"Well, Ahmed, I've only seen you shoot but that was amazing. Where did you learn that?"

"Garages, sir." There was another snigger from Bailey's direction.

"And you." The sniggering stopped. "Robert, is it? You made some great saves tonight, even if this lad did beat you from the halfway line."

Wasim turned to find Bailey smiling again. But this time it was only with his mouth and Wasim couldn't avoid a pair of icy eyes somehow finding his own.

"What was that… Saturday?" It was a man in a suit and a very smart coat. The man shook Mr Dawson's hand. "Brian Bailey. This young man's father, for my sins." He put a proud arm on Robert's shoulder.

"I've been picked for Woodley Wanderers," Robert said.

"Well, a trial match anyway," Mr Dawson said.

Bailey's dad seemed to grow a foot taller and his grip on Robert's shoulder must have hurt.

"Great. Well, I know a bit about the game myself so if you need any help…"

Mr Dawson politely told him that he didn't need any. Then Bailey was made to say thank you to Mr Dawson while his dad snatched the last cone from Wasim and put it into the boot, just to look helpful.

"See you Saturday," Mr Bailey smiled, and with a last wave he was off through the gates with his son following.

"See you, Charles," Bailey sneered back, making it obvious that he wasn't talking to Wasim.

Chapter Five

The Wanderers!

"Good, eh, Waz?"

"Yeah, good."

They were on their way back to Wasim's now. They'd got to Charles's house but no one was in for him to give the good news to. So they were going to Wasim's, just to keep talking about it and to tell his mum and dad together.

"Mint, eh, Waz?"

"Yeah, mint," Wasim replied. And it was mint. He was a Wanderer. That meant somebody who could go anywhere, somebody everybody liked. A Wanderer! They were running now, Charles and Wasim, too excited to walk. Maybe he wasn't a nothing… maybe he was a something, just like he always used to feel. Like Dad made him feel when he went to the mosque with the men. Like he'd always felt before Bailey and the crawling around on the corridor floor and the hiding at breaks. Wasim stopped running as it all came back.

"And tops," Charles shouted.

"Yeah, it's tops." Wasim wasn't listening really. He was thinking about the corridors.

"No. Their tops." Charles slowed down. "The tops – tracky tops. Red and black with your name and Wanderer printed on the back."

Wasim stopped too. Now he was listening. The tops… oh yes, the Wanderers tracksuit tops. They were at the garages already and he was almost feeling sorry for the old Wasim, the Wasim before he was a Woodley Wanderer – or nearly one, anyway. To think that before today he had actually thought playing down here with Dad and Atif was real football.

"They give you one – you know, after you get signed on. Then it's yours to keep. We'll have the same. We'll wear 'em for PE and…"

But Wasim was just seeing that

black and red top on his desk before
Teamwork 10,000 next week. They'd all
see it. They'd all see Ahmed –
Wanderer on the back and number nine
or something with it. Then they'd all
know it wasn't the old Wasim any
more. Wasim who got his name on the
board for shouting out, Wasim who did
'special' work with Mrs Hussein on
Wednesdays, Wasim whose name the
supply teachers couldn't say properly.

He started to run, and he wasn't Wasim who wore a PE vest for Teamwork 10,000. No! Now he'd be Number Nine – Ahmed. Now he'd be something different, because now he was Wasim the Wanderer.

● ● ●

"Come on. Hurry, Wasim."

Mum was worried about him coming in so late and he was being rushed to the bath and then in to get dressed before he had time to talk about anything, even his goal. It wasn't until he saw the clothes hanging up that he remembered about lessons at the mosque.

Tonight, like most nights, Wasim

would dress in his shalwar trousers and *kameez* shirt and go along with the other children to sit inside the tiny classroom and learn from the Koran.

Dad hated them to be late and so it wasn't until they were in the car that Wasim, his face scrubbed clean, got the news out.

"My son, one of the Woodley Wanderers?" Dad actually took his hand off the wheel and turned round when Wasim told him. Mum grabbed at the wheel and tutted. But when Dad was safely driving again, the smile half-hidden by her sari gave Wasim the same glow as Dad's shining eyes in the driving mirror.

And then with drips of rain sliding down the car window and only the shop lights to give away the smile fighting his lips, Wasim began to look forward to tomorrow. Tomorrow – his first full day as Number Nine – Ahmed.

Chapter Six

Wasim had it right. Being a Woodley Wanderer was brilliant. Mr Abbott had started it off as soon as he came into class with a letter for Mrs Scott.

"Well, Wasim?" he said in front of everybody, and Wasim thought he was in trouble. "What did Mum and Dad think, then? Woodley Wanderers, eh?"

"Pleased," was all Wasim managed to squeeze out through his grin.

Playtime was what Wasim was really

looking forward to and it was brilliant. Brilliant being called over to the Year Six pitch and being one of the first picked. Brilliant when everyone asked if he'd got his top yet. Brilliant when he told someone in Mr Wright's class where to stand for the kick-off, and they actually went there! Brilliant hearing someone say, "You mark Wasim."

Brilliant… until Robert Bailey toe-punted a ball right in his face and knocked the lens out of his glasses so that Wasim had to spend the rest of break looking for it and then going in to get his frames fixed.

"It was an accident, Miss," Robert Bailey said to the teacher on duty.

"Well, I hope so because I'm sure

we haven't got anyone at our school who would deliberately hurt somebody like that."

But the smirk on Bailey's face once Miss Pollitt went back to wiping noses and doing up shoelaces told Wasim a different story. Yet Wasim sensed that it wasn't just one of his lenses that had gone missing. There had been a feeling like a boulder in his tummy since the day Mr Abbott had taken Robert Bailey's ball … And now it wasn't quite so heavy.

"So?" Wasim shouted to the world, and he didn't know why, but he was laughing.

• • •

Dad had been all ready for a game down by the garages that evening and Wasim could tell he was disappointed.

"Wasim has asked if he can go training with his friend at the park," said Mum, looking a bit worried. Dad had stopped work to play and he only had half an hour, but he would have to understand.

"It's proper football. I can't play by the garages now. I've got to get real training on a real pitch," Wasim told him.

Dad gave an 'I give up' look which meant Wasim could go, and Mum said he had to be back before it even started to get dark.

Wasim sprinted round to Charles's house, trying to get so out of breath that he couldn't feel the guilty tickle in his stomach. Dad would understand, especially when he saw that Wanderers kit on Saturday.

● ● ●

"Bagsie in net!" Charles booted the ball high over the tennis courts and raced towards the football pitches. "Three and in."

But Charles stopped and Wasim followed his disappointed gaze. The goal at the far end had some big kids – fourteen, fifteen year olds – playing in it. And at this end… Wasim couldn't believe it! There, in his best England goalkeeper's kit, was Robert Bailey. Robert's dad was in a tracksuit and baseball cap. He was almost purple and he was screaming at Bailey.

"Useless! Keep your eyes on it. Useless!" He stormed up to the goalkeeper and shook him hard. "No chance on Saturday, no chance at all. Keep those eyes on it

53

and chest behind it. Now, again."

Mr Bailey snatched the ball from his silent son and stalked back to the penalty spot. Wasim and Charles quickly put their ball down and passed it in case he thought they were looking at him.

"NO!" This was a scream and even the lads at the far end stopped their game. "Hold on to it!"

The ball had gone through the posts and was heading right for them. Both Wasim and Charles put their heads down and pretended to pass even more carefully.

Bailey had came over to get the ball and Wasim looked up. "What are you looking at, Ahmed?"

It was then that Wasim realised.

He'd known it since break time really, but now he was sure. He wasn't scared of Robert Bailey. Not after he'd gone back out with his glasses smashed and his whole face one huge sting. What more was there?

Bailey wasn't the Robert Bailey he'd been dreading any more. Not now it had happened. Not now Bailey had actually hurt him and it wasn't just a threat building up in Wasim's tummy.

"Come on, Robert!" The shout from the pitch made the crows in the big conker tree take off. Robert ran to where the ball had come to rest against the tennis fence and then half-walked, half-ran back to the man glaring at him with his hands on his hips. But it was too late. He was coming over to them.

"Do you know these lads?" he asked his son.

"Sort of," Bailey whispered.

And before Wasim could signal him to shut up, Charles had piped up, "We're in it on Saturday as well. You saw us at school."

"Oh yes." Mr Bailey seemed to have forgotten them. "Right, well, come over and we'll practise some crosses."

Not being scared of Bailey was one thing, but playing with him at the park?

They crossed the ball about fifty times and Bailey caught most of them. When he missed, though, they all had to wait for five minutes while Mr Bailey shouted about positioning, timing and how Robert might as well have margarine on his hands instead of thirty-pound international goalkeeper's gloves.

Then it was shots. Charles took those and Wasim sat on the freezing mud while Robert pulled off some good saves.

"OK, son, you take one."

Wasim wasn't in the mood now, but once the ball came rolling out to him he thought of how hard Bailey had punted the ball into his face at break, and he really hit it. It was one of his specials. Hard, low and then rising at the last second into where the net would have been if there was one. Robert Bailey hadn't moved. It was unstoppable.

"Nice one, Waz," Charles said.

"Rubbish!"

Wasim stopped his high fives celebrations with Charles, but it wasn't him Mr Bailey was shouting at.

"Dive, you great cissy. What, are you scared of the thing? Look he's only a…"

The man looked at Wasim and took a breath while Wasim waited to hear what he 'only' was. Mr Bailey ended up not saying anything Wasim could hear and he walked away holding his head, making a big show of keeping his temper.

Wasim thought he'd better get the ball and he set off. He had to walk right past a chalk-faced

Robert Bailey and he waited for something. A little kick, a trip, a sneer, at least. But the boy was just standing looking at the ground and his lips hardly seemed to move.

"He could have been a professional, my dad."

Had he heard right? Bailey making excuses for what his dad was like? Wasim slowed but he didn't know if he was supposed to say anything, so he walked on and got the ball.

Mr Bailey was calm enough to talk by the time Wasim got back. "Right – chips. Save a chip shot and it makes it look good … even if a keeper is rubbish."

Wasim wanted to go home. Pro or not, Bailey's dad was way over the top

and it was getting dark. Just to think
he could have had a normal game at
the garages.

"Just five more minutes. Give Rob
some chips in, eh?"

Wasim and Charles shrugged and
got ready while Mr Bailey went through
a sort of ballet dance with his son.

"If you want to play for Woodley
Wanderers, you make it look good.
Eye on the ball, and it's step, step back,
jump and tap over. OK boys, chip
a high one in. Right, Robert, say it!

Bailey mumbled something.

"SAY IT!" The shout
bounced around the park.

"Step, step back,
jump and tap over."

"No! It's eye on

the ball, step, step back, jump and tap over."

Robert finally said it right. And for the next half an hour, from when Wasim floated his first high ball under the crossbar and the keeper arched his back and tapped it over, he really did make it look brilliant. It was 'Eye on the ball, step, step back, jump and tap over...' until it was too dark to see.

Chapter Seven

It was Saturday afternoon at Woodley Park, the home of Woodley Wanderers Football Club. Nans held coats, swings swung and a roundabout squeaked.

Away from the play area, boys in red and black kicked balls high over the wooden changing rooms and grown ups talked about a good home win and a 'cheating' ref last week.

Wasim had a big jumper over his PE kit. This would be the last time.

After today he'd have a real tracksuit,
one he'd earned. Better than any of
those kits the other kids in school
wore every day.

Lost in the new crowd, neither
Charles nor Wasim said a word and
none of the tall, confident boys with
WANDERER on their backs said a word

to them. On the other side of the group of parents stood Robert Bailey, his dad pacing up and down, barking something into a mobile phone.

Wasim watched the car park. Would his dad finish at work and get here in time? Would Mr Dawson bring three new tracksuits – one of them saying Ahmed on the back?

Finally a white car nosed its way into an empty space in the car park. It was Mr Dawson's, not Dad's, and Wasim stood back while the manager was surrounded by a gang of baying boys asking what positions they'd be in, and almost as many pestering dads. Wasim and Charles kept a safe distance.

"OK," Mr Dawson smiled, holding up the key to the dressing room.

"Let's get in and I'll sort you out."

The door opened and the howling pack pushed through. Nobody listened or cared what anybody else was saying or doing. Charles nudged Wasim forward but Wasim stood firm. This was one time when he did not want to be first.

"Right." Then Mr Dawson noticed them. "Whitefield can't play us today so it's a friendly against the Under-Twelves."

Under-Twelves – Bailey's age. Wasim would be playing against Bailey!

"I'm using it as a sort of trial. We've got a couple of new lads to look at." Mr Dawson pointed. "Charles here – midfielder, outstanding player, and, er…" Wasim waited for him to get it right, "and, er… Wasim. I've not seen much of young Wasim but he's got a shot like a mule."

Wasim tried to grin but his mouth was too dry.

"I'm also looking at a new keeper for the Under-Twelves, so try him out. Plenty of shots…"

● ● ●

The real stuff began with a warm-up
outside, where Wasim tried to show
how fast he could be, and then it was
all back inside. The hut was a proper
dressing room and when Wasim saw
the bench going down the middle with
the red and black shirts hanging above
it, he knew that this was real football
and that he could become part of it
if he did well today.

Wasim the Wanderer pulled on a
shirt and felt the nylon slide over his
hair and his dreams come true.

Chapter Eight

"OK, quiet lads."

Mr Dawson clapped and this time there was quiet. The mums and dads were locked outside and there was a change. The smile had gone, the jokes had gone. Mr Dawson wanted to win this game, even if it was only a friendly against the Under-Twelves. It was how Wasim's dad was just before they got to the mosque – serious.

Wasim's eyes watered with the

fumes from the Raelgex muscle cream that the others had rubbed into their legs. He heard the smack of chewing gum in mouths and the odd clack of a boot which had dared to stir and risk breaking the manager's concentration.

This *was* the mosque for Mr Dawson. Football was his religion.

Wasim tried to imagine booting a ball about in the garages or in the playground. Was it the same thing?

"You are all Wanderers. Woodley Wanderers. You and you!" Wasim and

Charles sat upright. The finger was pointing at them. "Today you could become Wanderers. Charles, you'll be in midfield with Trevor. Wasim, you'll be up front. Lots of running. Support the front two. Johnny, you'll drop down to sub. Give Wasim a game. OK?" There was a silence again. "OK, Johnny?"

"Yeah!" It wasn't OK and Wasim felt two holes where Johnny, whoever he was, burned him with a glare.

Then the door was opened, light shafted in and it was, "Go on, lads. Do it for the Wanderers."

Wasim stood and sprinted into the light as fast as his legs would carry him. He heard the claps. He saw the crowd around the pitch and there, with a smile the size of Woodley Park, he saw

his dad and next to him Atif and Uncle
Zan. Wasim's chest grew and a tickly
feeling in his stomach sent him
sprinting even faster than the others
towards the halfway line and a practice
ball. He booted one to Charles, sprinted

to get it, and then he heard a whistle.

"Captains." The coin was tossed. "Swap ends."

Wasim just turned round but the goalkeepers had to go the whole length of the pitch. And here, walking towards him slowly, gum chewing, cap and gloves in his hands, came Robert Bailey, trying his best to look like the cock of the roost he was in the school playground.

"Hurry up, Robert!"

It was Mr Bailey again. Robert gave a start, dropped his gloves, fumbled to pick them up and had to run past Wasim. Some of the Under-Twelves in the Wanderer white Away kit were laughing at him.

The whistle went and, with a last

glance over at Dad, Wasim tried to get the hard look on his face that the others had.

"Come on, reds!"

"Go on, lad."

The ball was coming to him and so was a great big kid in white. Wasim tried to move and he turned nicely. But nerves meant that his legs hadn't been told and they stayed still. Come on… One leg moved… finally… out of the mud and towards the shiny white ball. Now the other leg got going and Wasim was on his way towards being picked properly for the Wanderers and earning the tracksuit top that would make him king of Year Five on Monday.

Oohf! A white shirt hit him and Wasim felt himself falling and saw the ball disappear. There was a groan from the crowd.

"Oh nice. Well done!"

Wasim on hands and knees looked up in hope. But the praise wasn't for him. Charles, his wavy blonde hair bouncing and face fixed, had won the ball with a crunching tackle on the boy twice his size. Now he was bringing it forward for the reds again, his eyes flashing and nodding, "Come on, come on."

Wasim, just making it up on to his feet, knew what he meant. Charles was

going to help him out but Wasim didn't want it… not yet.

"Waz.. go…" Charles was ready to side foot one of his hard but perfect passes to Wasim. "Come on… move!"

Charles was being chased by three white shirts now and his eyes were shouting at Wasim to come and get the ball. Finally, Wasim pulled himself together, looked around for white shirts – none – and was ready for the pass.

It came… perfect… and Wasim was ready to go.

WHACK!

Where did that come from? He'd checked that he wasn't marked. And then he saw. It was a red shirt who had taken the ball, one of his own players… He'd taken too long and

so now he wasn't going to get it.
He chased to keep up, but the red
Wanderers had swarmed past him and
were on the edge of the area. There
were two quick passes, a shout of
"Out, Robert" from the side and then
a shot... straight at the goalkeeper.

Wasim turned away but a groan and
a cheer had him spinning back round.
Robert Bailey held his head in his
hands, and the reds were dancing with
delight. The ball must have gone
straight through the keeper's legs.

"TWIT!" came that voice from the
side, and even the baying Wanderer
parents were shocked into silence.

Chapter Nine

For Wasim, it was the nightmare
of Teamwork 10,000 all over again.
He was pushed out to the side of the
field and after that one mistake he
wasn't going to get a touch. He
sprinted up and down the touchline
just centimetres from all of the
Wanderer tracksuits on the grass. His
chances of getting one of those were
disappearing with every second,
especially as the substitutes had started

warming up.

At least without the ball he wasn't making any more mistakes. Not like Robert Bailey. He had gone to pieces. He couldn't hold a pass back. There was his dad, behind the goal now, shouting, holding his head, looking to the heavens and shaking a fist at every drop and fumble.

There was a big clap from the line. Charles was playing a blinder and he had the ball again. "Oh nice, Charles," purred Mr Dawson. "OK, Johnny. Next stop I'll bring you on and give Wasim a rest."

That was it. Wasim felt a sort of pang in his chest and found his legs slowing as he ran forward with the play, hoping for the hundredth time that the ball would be passed out to him.

"Come on, Waz, move." Charles still had it, and once again was heading for goal and being chased by three white shirts and bigger, faster boys.

"Go, Wasim!" But it was too late. Wasim wasn't moving quickly enough. Charles would have to do it on his own and there was a groan from the side and an angry flash of Charles's blue eyes as the big midfielders hammered into him and he went down. Wasim should have called for it, should have given him something to aim at, should have…

But then came the noise that was telling the story of the match again. Groans, shouts and even a laugh this

time. The two whites had tripped over
Charles and they were down in the
mud with him. So there was the ball
sitting in the middle of the pitch. And
now, like a dial being turned up, came
the noise – rising, rising. Wasim was
in a perfect position to bring the ball
forward and release the front players.

With their arms raised like radio aerials, they were speeding down opposite sides of the pitch, taking the defenders with them and freeing up the middle.

Wasim could see what had opened up. He could hear the boys on the wings screaming for a pass and he could see an empty green tunnel to goal.

"GO!" he could hear Uncle Zan shout, and Wasim went.

He went fast. There was no one to stop him. The defenders had spotted too late that he was going for goal and now the grown-ups supporting the Under-Twelves were screaming at them.

They were eleven years old. How could they have let a forward get through like that?

Wasim was at the edge of the penalty box with only the keeper to beat. Only the keeper. Wasim was where he had only dreamed of being, right there with a chance of a Wasim shot, a Wasim cannon ball, a bulging net and a Wanderers tracksuit. Only the keeper to beat. Only Robert Bailey.

"Get out to him, you soft lump of lard!"

And slowly off of his line came Robert.

Wasim decided which side of the net to blast it. One last tap, the plant of his foot, one last look up to see which way Bailey thought he would put it.

It was the look up that did it.

Wasim's eyes met Robert Bailey's — and saw pure fear. Bailey was petrified and suddenly it was like being back in the school corridor. They were facing each other, but this time it was Bailey having to wait to see which way he was going to be hurt and it was Wasim going to do the hurting. It wouldn't be a fist, though. It would be a screamer into the roof of the net with Bailey left stranded, his dad shouting and another goalkeeper picked for the Wanderers.

"Get out to him, you soft nellie, Robert."

Wasim had one more glance at the haunted eyes, welling with tears now. He had one more second of being a Bailey coming down the corridor ready to hurt someone. And because Wasim Ahmed didn't have a dad like Robert Bailey's and because Wasim Ahmed would never purposefully hurt anybody, he had only one more second of Woodley Wanderers.

He chipped it.

Wasim didn't blast it. He chipped it and the goalkeeper's red eyes emptied their tears on to his cheeks and filled instead with surprise. Then the surprise turned to memory – 'Eye on the ball, step, step back, jump and tap over.'

Robert Bailey kept his eye on the ball, stepped, stepped back, jumped, and tipped the floating ball over the top of the crossbar. Both sides of the pitch cheered what looked like the best save they'd ever seen down at

Woodley Park.

Wasim ran to the side. He tapped hands with Johnny the sub, left his shirt in the wooden hut and went home.

Chapter Ten

Dad and Shamaila were Chelsea, Wasim and Atif were United. It was great! Garage doors knew that kids didn't make mistakes on purpose and so they never shouted. Sometimes, though, when Wasim scored one of his scorchers, it sounded as though they were clapping.

Wasim put his foot on the ball when Charles and Robert turned the corner. He had tried to work out how he'd be able to look as if he didn't care when he next saw them. But still he couldn't get his breathing right as they ran over, each swinging a plastic sports-shop bag that could only be holding a black Wanderers top.

"Can we have a game?"

Mr Ahmed waited for Wasim's tiny nod before he said, "Of course."

Charles tried to help with the sudden silence as the pair put down their plastic bags. "Hey, Waz... Mr Dawson said he might have another look at you at Teamwork on Wednesday... You coming?"

"Dunno," Wasim said, because he was looking around at the garages, at his brother and sister, at Dad out of breath, and then up at old Mr Holloway

slurping a cup of tea on his balcony.
He was looking at two plastic bags and
thinking about real football where you
got taken off; where only winning, only
points mattered. And he didn't care.
He really didn't care.

"You can be on my team on
Wednesday," said Robert.

It was Robert Bailey, in goal in the
United garage. Wasim drew back his
foot and *bhouff*, the ball left his foot
like a tornado and made a dent a metre
wide in the metal next to Bailey's head.

"Minter!" Mr Holloway shouted.

Read about Wasim's swimming skills in

Wasim One-Star

CHRIS ASHLEY

Chris Ashley is football mad and only
started writing once he was too old to play.
"It was my back that went first," Chris explains.
"I was a goalkeeper and constantly picking the ball
out of the net became too much of a strain."

Chris is a Londoner but works as a headteacher
in the north of England, and it is in the classroom
that he finds many of the characters for
his stories. Wasim, who also appears in
Wasim One-Star, is his favourite.

Also available from
Frances Lincoln Children's Books

Wasim One-Star

Chris Ashley
Illustrated by Kate Pankhurst

Wasim wants to be a One-Star swimmer.
But when the day comes to take the plunge,
Wasim's up to his neck in trouble. When Wasim
gets ordered out of the pool for talking to the
new boy, Wayne, his chances of getting his
One Star vanish. Will Wasim be a star
or must he wait until next year for
his chance to shine?

ISBN 978-1-84507-775-4

Dear Whiskers

Ann Whitehead Nagda
Illustrated by Stephanie Roth

Everyone in Jenny's class has to write a letter to
someone in another class. Only you have to pretend
to be a mouse! Jenny thinks the whole thing
is really silly... until her penfriend writes back.
There is something mysterious about Jenny's
penfriend. Will Jenny discover her secret?

ISBN: 978-1-84507-563-7

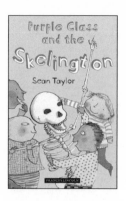

Purple Class and the Skelington

Sean Taylor
Illustrated by Helen Bate

Meet Purple Class – there is Jamal who often
forgets his reading book, Ivette who is the best
in the class at everything, Yasmin who is sick on
every school trip, Jodie who owns a crazy
snake called Slinkypants, Leon who is great
at rope-swinging, Shea who knows all about
blood-sucking slugs and Zina who makes a rather
disturbing discovery in the teacher's chair...

ISBN: 978-1-84507-377-0

Purple Class and the Flying Spider

Sean Taylor
Illustrated by Helen Bate

Purple Class are back in four new school stories!
Leon has managed to lose 30 violins, much to
the horror of the violin teacher; Jodie thinks
she has uncovered an unexploded bomb in
the vegetable patch; Shea has allowed Bad Boy,
Purple Class's guinea pig to escape; and Ivette
has discovered a scary flying spider,
just in time for Parents' Evening!

ISBN 978-1-84507-627-6